For everyone I've blown my top at. —A.D.

For Prithvi, my sweet laddu. —A.A.

DON'T BLOW YOUR TOP!

WRITTEN BY **AME DYCKMAN**

ILLUSTRATED BY **ABHI ALWAR**

ORCHARD BOOKS

An Imprint of Scholastic Inc.

New York

It was a beautiful day in Paradise.

Big Volcano was happy.

Little Volcano was happy.

Until —

Something unexpected happened.

Would Little Volcano . . .
BLOW THEIR TOP?

It happened before.

But Little Volcano was older now.

They breathed.

They counted.
They counted all the way to:

They both thought happy thoughts.

And . . .

It worked!
Little Volcano *didn't* blow their top!

Until —

Something unexpected happened *again*. Twice!

But *this* time . . .

After a while, Little Volcano said:

Big Volcano said:

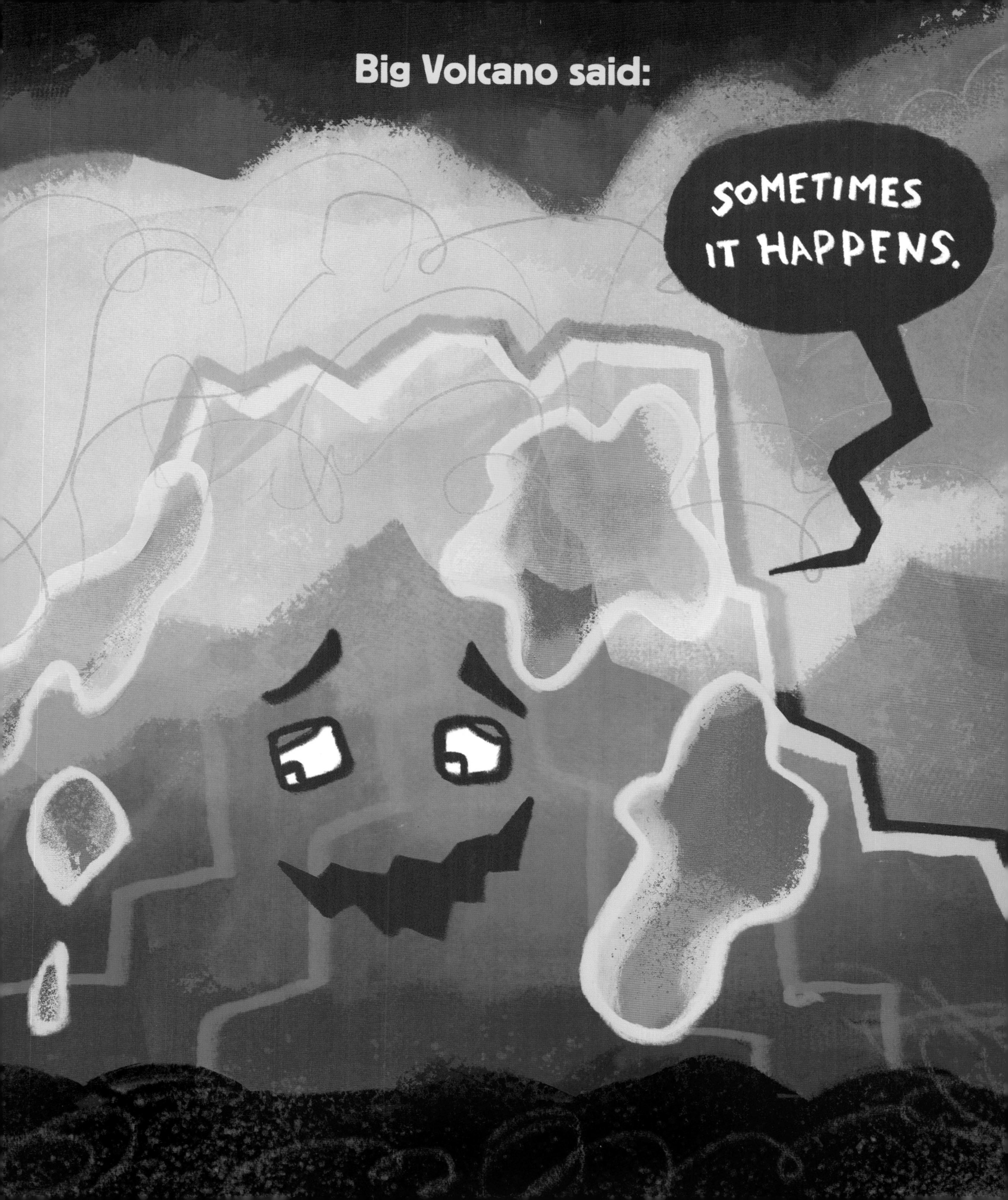

Little Volcano took a deep breath and said:

I'M SORRY.

Big Volcano said:

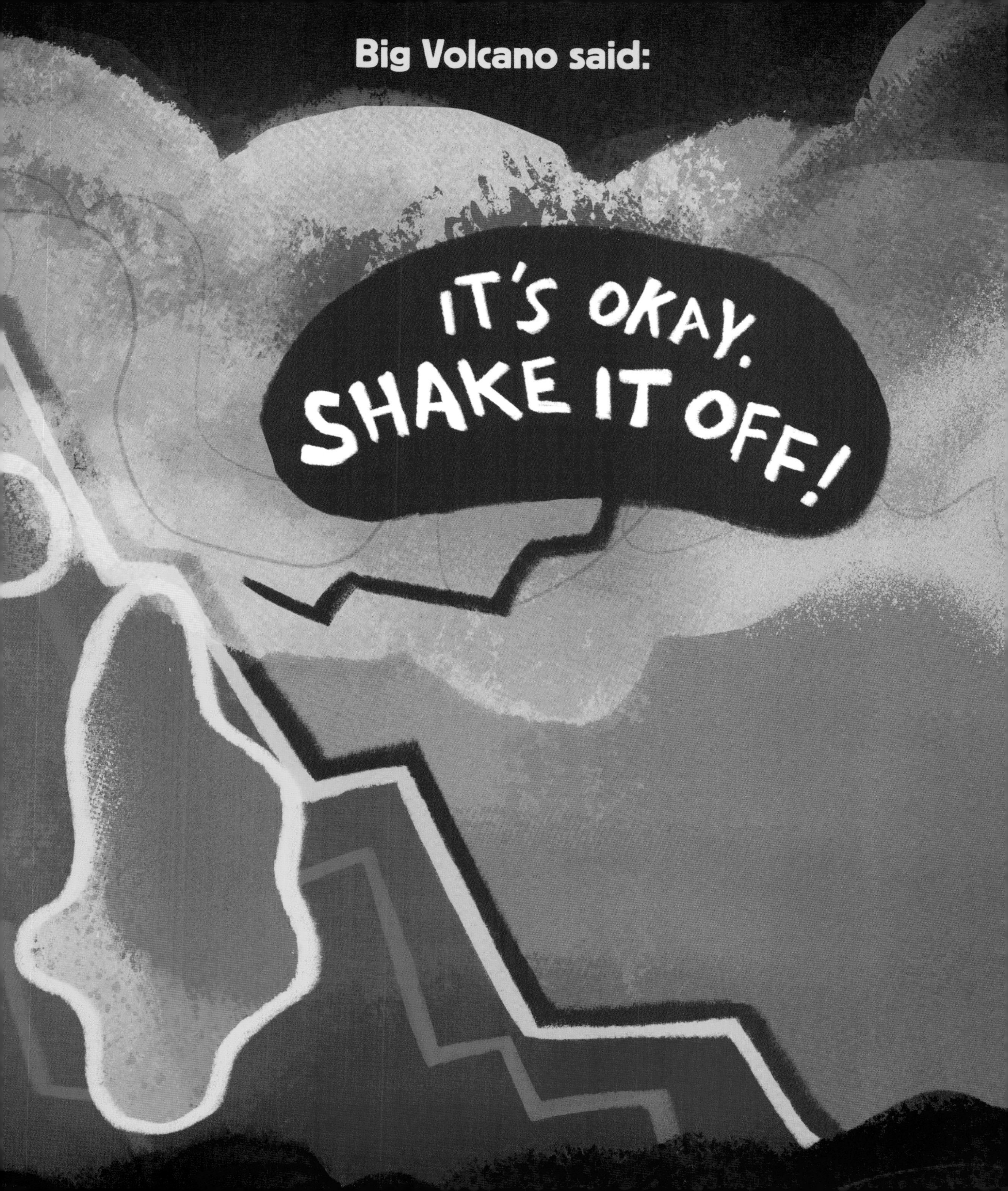

Then once again . . .

It was a beautiful day in Paradise.

Little Volcano was happy.
Big Volcano was happy.
Until —

This time, it was Little Volcano who said:

BREATHE.

COUNT.

HAPPY THOUGHTS.

And . . .

It worked.